The Messy Family

Written by
Katherine Pebley O'Neal

Illustrated by
Laura Huliska-Beith

ZONDERkidz

ZONDERVAN.com/
AUTHORTRACKER
follow your favorite authors

You are already clean because of the word I have spoken to you.
— John 15:3

The Messy Family
Copyright © 2008 by Katherine Pebley O'Neal
Illustrations © 2008 by Laura Huliska-Beith

Requests for information should be addressed to:
Zonderkidz, Grand Rapids, Michigan 49530

Library of Congress Cataloging-in-Publication Data

   O'Neal, Katherine Pebley.
The Messy family / by Katherine Pebley O'Neal ; [illustrations by
 Laura Huliska-Beith].
   p. cm.
   Summary: Mr. and Mrs. Messy and their sons, Dusty and Rusty,
do their best to tidy up before guests arrive, but while hiding dirty
dishes and stashing toys they make some discoveries—including
that their friends feel welcome despite the mess.
   ISBN-13: 978-0-310-70985-5 (printed hardcover)
   ISBN-10: 0-310-70985-7 (printed hardcover)
   [1. Orderliness–Fiction. 2. Friendship–Fiction. 3. Family life
–Fiction.] I. Huliska-Beith, Laura, ill. II. Title.
PZ7.O548938Mes 2008

[E]–dc22   2005036441

All Scripture quotations unless otherwise noted are taken from the *Holy Bible: New
International Version*®. NIV®. Copyright © 1973, 1978, 1984 by International Bible
Society. Used by permission of Zondervan. All rights reserved.

Zonderkidz is a trademark of Zondervan.

Art direction & Design: Merit Alderink
Editor: Amy DeVries

Printed in China

08 09 10 11 • 6 5 4 3 2 1

To Corey, Connor, Evan, and Lainey,
who are usually too messy.

-K.P.O.

For Mom and Dad:
Thank you for all the love and patience
you gave your loud and messy children!

-L.H.B.

"Scrub the table till it sparkles." Mrs. Messy sang.
"Sweep the kitchen till it shines." called Mr. Messy.
"Dust the corners till they're spotless." chimed in Rusty and Dusty.
"We'll tidy up the house!" they all said together.

"Company's coming. We have a lot to do," exclaimed Mrs. Messy. Everyone worked hard.

Mr. and Mrs. Messy stashed dishes in the closets. The twins shoved toys and books under their beds.

Mr. Messy rolled up his sleeves. "We're making good progress," he said.

"It does look better already!" Mrs. Messy noticed.

The contents of Dusty's closet shelf
fell on top of him. "Agh!" he shrieked.

But Rusty did not rush to help him. He stood
still in the corner of the room. "Stop cleaning!"
he cried. "Look what I almost dusted away."
"Wow," said Dusty. "That's a really big web."

A little while later, Dusty had a discovery of his own.

"Hey, look what I found under the bed!" called Dusty.
"Kittens!" Rusty cried. "Mopsy had kittens!"
"It's a very good thing I didn't clean under there," said Dusty.
Mrs. Messy smiled. "Who knows how many of God's creatures may be making their homes with us," she said.

"Oh, it's time for your soccer game," exclaimed Mrs. Messy, looking at her watch.

"And we still have errands to run," Mr. Messy said. "I'm afraid there's no time to finish cleaning the house."

"Our friends will have to take us as they find us— as usual," Mrs. Messy replied.

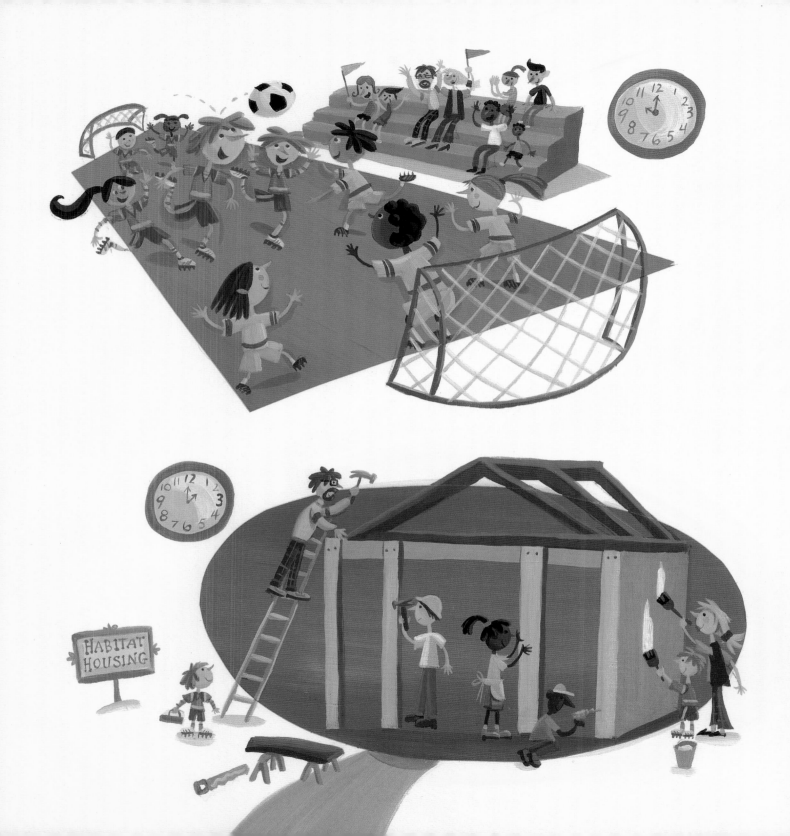

HABITAT
HOUSING

Mr. and Mrs. Albright and their son, Tom, came over for dinner that night.

"Thank you for inviting us," Mrs. Albright said as they gathered around the table.

"The chicken smells delicious!" said Mr. Albright.

"We were busy all day," Mrs. Messy said with a sigh, looking at the stacks of dishes in the kitchen. "I apologize for the mess."

"Not to worry. We love your home because we always feel so welcome here," said Mrs. Albright.

Everyone bowed their heads as Mr. Messy said grace. "Dear Lord, thank you for our friends. May all those who come to our home be blessed. And please bless this food. Amen."

After dinner, Dusty, Rusty, and Tom made a fort using all the cushions from the living room furniture.

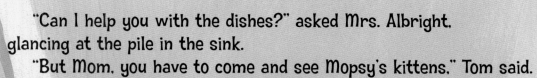

"Can I help you with the dishes?" asked Mrs. Albright, glancing at the pile in the sink.

"But Mom, you have to come and see Mopsy's kittens," Tom said.

"Kittens?" Mrs. Albright asked with a smile.

"Yes, let's go see them. The dishes can wait," said Mrs. Messy, relieved.

And they all went upstairs to look for Mopsy
and her family under the bed.